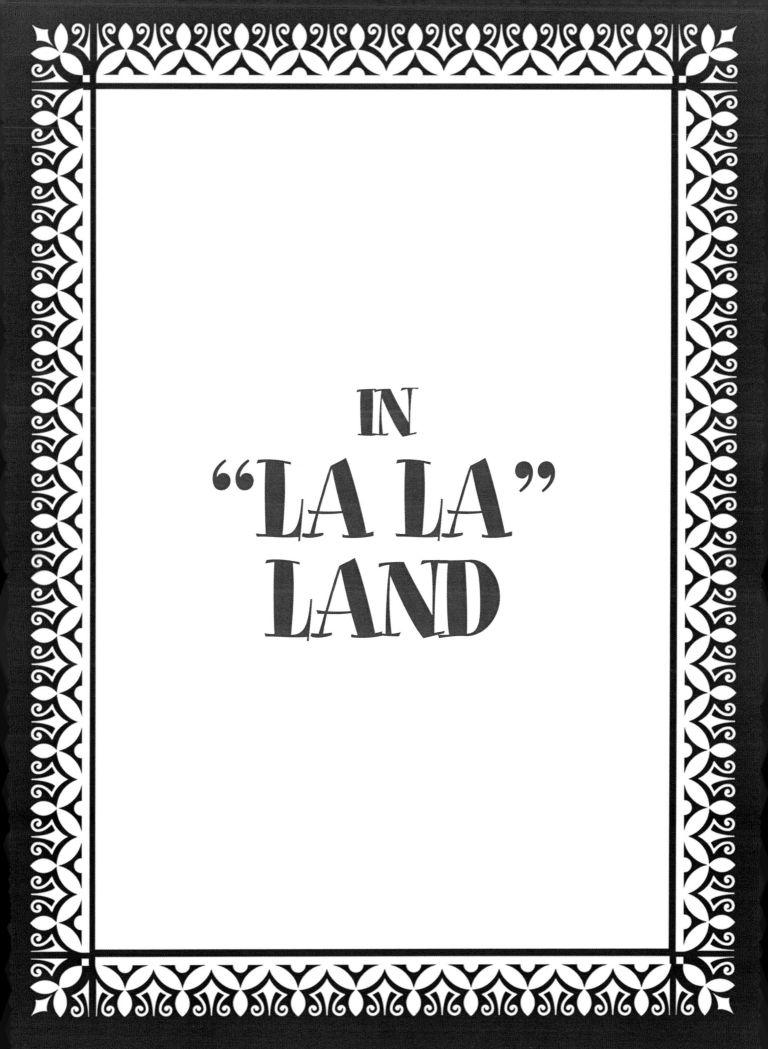

IN "LA LA" LAND

To order additional copies of this book, contact:
Xlibris
1-888-795-4274
www.Xlibris.com
Orders@Xlibris.com

Illustrated by
Najah Clemmons

DEDICATION

This book is dedicated to my Baby Brother Victor for not only sharing, but enjoying my childish dreams; My Brother Marcelle for laughing "out loud" with me and for pushing me to finish; My Daddy Ralph for giving me his sense of humor and for cheering loudly at my "Doll Baby Shows", the very beginning of my creativity; and my Mommie Frances for believing in everything I do no matter how crazy it sounds; and also for providing dinner after the "Doll Baby Shows" which she watched as well. I Love you All!!

Theme Song

Felecia R. Hough
Arranged by Gail Hall

Theme Song

Raindrops are golden
When small eyes behold them
Leaves become dollars
When small hands unfold them

Pools can be rivers
Ponds, beaches and such . . .
Waterfalls, fountains yes little means much.

By napping or sleeping
By night or by day
Every child gets there in his or her way.

Some may count sheep
Or count waves from the sand
All are well happy and free . . .
In "La La" Land.

Introduction

Once upon a time there was a princess
who lived in a very small town.

Princess Fee was her name and it
Wasn't too often that she wore a frown.

For she had a secret that only she knew
And now she asked me to share it with you.

Whenever she was bored and could find nothing to do
She used her special gift called "Imagination".
Do you know how to use yours too?

I really hope so because she had lots of fun
And you'll feel so much better after each
Adventure is done.

" THE ROYAL TEA PARTY"

Objective:

This fantasy short story is designed to help children imagine a special party that would honor good behavior and achievement by featuring all of their favorite people, colors, sounds, foods, etc.

Suggestion:

Parents or teachers can use this story to learn whom, or what is dearest and most important to each child individually and collectively. In addition, this story can be used to gather ideas for ways to reward, or discipline by granting, or withholding these favorite and most cherished items.

Once upon a time . . . In La La Land, it was time for the Royal Tea Party! Let's get ready, for this is a celebration! Oh what a wonderful, colorful and beautiful occasion! For this was not just any old tea party; this was the greatest, most magnificent, truly significant tea party of them all! At this tea party and only this tea party, were the most special and the best behaved and for the most deserving were special seats saved!

Would you like to go? Well you know the way. Close your eyes and use your imagination, for it's your golden good kid invitation.

As you push open the great big doors and enter the great big room, you hear a very loud noise and a very big boom! Just relax. You do not have to fear, there is never anything scary here. It's just Big Boy, Pretty Bear, Beauty, and Puppy too! They were planning an extra surprise for you! Roof! Roof! Roof! What are they saying? You'll know soon, but here is a hint. They were trying to bring you a big balloon. Did you guess? Can you figure it out? What is all the commotion about?

Ta Da! Take a look around. All of your favorite colors and all of your favorite sounds! All of your favorite people and all of your favorite pets. Just as if you had won a hundred thousand kazillion bets! **(Stop and ask children who do they see or what do they hear?)**

For this is why the "Royal Tea Party" is so fantastic and so grand. This is also why Princess Fee and Lady Erica always invite as many as they can! Can you smell the cup cakes, the popcorn and chocolate candy? Can you feel the gentle breeze? If not, the fun cool zone is really handy! Can you taste that big old juicy pickle that did not even cost you a nickel? Quickly, find your special table. Find the balloon that is your favorite color; **remember this was your very first clue.** You see, once you're at the Royal Tea Party, how you have fun and whom you have fun with is totally up to you!

"THE ROYAL GERM WAR"

Objective:

This short story is designed to present a potentially real life conflict that a child may encounter. While the action demonstrates an imaginative solution to help their playmate, embedded in the story are ways to prevent the spread of germs and the importance of medicinal use with safety, and the power of team work.

Suggestion:

At bedtime, or naptime this story can be used to explain why playmates may be sick or, absent. This story can be used to precede a lesson on germs, hand washing, medical professionals, immunizations, etc. Children could possibly re-enact the germ war by using water balloons and foam sprayers under close supervision. This story softens the tone of the term war, and demonstrates how an ugly term can really be used for good. With a twist of irony, it also gives children a better understanding of the title, war hero.

Once upon a time in "La La Land," Prince Jerl and Prince Mick came looking for Princess Fee. To their surprise she was still asleep. Of course everyone knew how she loved her naps, but this was not just any old day. It was Saturday, and they needed to practice for the Royal Kick Ball game later on that day.

What could be wrong with Princess Fee, they wondered as they sat on the porch swinging their little feet? "She has caught the flu", said Queen Fran to the worried little fellows.

"But how, and who threw it to her?" they said. "No, No, No young men, the flu is caused by a virus", answered Queen Fran.

"What's a virus?" they asked.

"A virus is a tiny, tiny bug called a germ. These germs float in the air when people do not cover their sneezes, and they hide on doorknobs when people do not wash their hands," explained Queen Fran.

"Ewwwh," said the little ones. "How is Lady Erica?" asked Prince Jerl. (Lady Erica is Princess Fee's very best friend and most loyal side kick.) "Lady Erica is not sick, but she's keeping Princess Fee company as usual. I'll be sure to tell them both that you came by," said Queen Fran.

"Yes mam," they said together as they dragged away terribly disappointed. At least they could hear Queen Fran singing the "Medicine song". It always helped them feel better about taking their medicine. Perhaps Princess Fee will soon be feeling better.

Medicine Song

Felecia R. Hough
Arranged by Gail Hall

MED --- I --- CINE MED --- I --- CINE MED --- I --- CINE

MED --- I --- CINE MAKES ME FEEL BET --- TER

MED --- I --- CINE MAKES ME FEEL STRONG BUT

I SHOULD NE --- VER TAKE MED --- I --- CINE WHEN

EV -- ER I AM A --- LONE WHEN

EV -- ER I'M SICK AND NEED MED --- I --- CINE MY

MOM SINGS THE MED --- I --- CINE SONG

MED --- I --- CINE MED --- I --- CINE MED --- I --- CINE

FADE OUT

MED --- I --- CINE MED --- I --- CINE MED --- I --- CINE

Song: "The Medicine Song"

Medicine, Medicine, Me-di-cine

Medicine, Medicine, Me-di-cine

Medicine makes me feel better

Medicine makes me feel strong

But I should never take medicine

Whenever I am alone.

Medicine makes me feel better

Medicine makes me feel strong

Whenever I'm sick and need medicine

My Mom sings the medicine song.

Medicine, medicine, me-di-cine

Medicine, medicine, me-di-cine

Princess Fee is an excellent kicker and even more so, she is a very good cousin. "There must be something we could do," said Prince Mick. " I have a plan" Prince Jerl replied. Let's have a Royal Germ War! Yeah that's it! We'll blast the whole kingdom squeaky clean and Princess Fee will surely get better. Do you want to help? Well close your eyes and prepare for blast off. Is your imagination ready? 10-9-8-7-6-5-4-3-2-1! Blast Off! **(Air Plane sounds; Ask children how their plane sounds.)**

Grip your wheel really tight and pull back. "Wooooo Hooooo," said Prince Jerl. "Isn't it beautiful up here?" " Yes it certainly is," said Prince Mick. Now, back to our mission. Let's go really high above the clouds so we can be sure to spot every one of those wicked germs. "All right Prince Mick, have you located a target yet," asked Prince Jerl. " Negative Prince Jerl, but I'm closing in on some very suspicious objects right now! Woa! They're dripping yicky, sticky, stinky, rinky, ishy, squishy goo!" "That must be those horrible germs," exclaimed Prince Jerl! Attack! **(make repeated shooting sounds… boom,plub,nuna nuna pow; ask children what are their shooting sounds?)**

"Did you get them Prince Jerl?" "No, I only did a little damage Prince Mick, but I'm preparing to launch our superkadupa alcohol lysol missile and that should do the trick. Just cover me with a couple of disinfectant gas bombs, ok"? " Ok, I've got you covered," said Prince Mick. "Here goes," he shouts as Prince Jerl releases the missile. (Pssshhhhh! Boom! Boom! Nuna Nuna Pow! Ka boom!) "I think we got them cuz!!" "Me too" replied Prince Mick. " All right prepare for landing." "Roger," said Prince Jerl. "Who's Roger?" asked Prince Mick. "You know, that's ok for airplane talk," Prince Jerl replied. " Ohhh… ok, I mean, roger." Oh No," shouted Prince Jerl! "What is it?" asked Prince Mick. " I'm running out of gas… we're in big trouble," said Prince Jerl. "Make that a double", Prince Mick added. May day, may day. Plane going down! **(Airplane sounds; Think fast: what could the Prince do to keep the plane from crashing?)**

"Breaker, breaker 1 – 9, this is Prince Wayne AKA Chocolate Thunder, can you hear me?" " Yes, this is Prince Jerl…Help!!!" " All right! Quick get your parachute, fasten it real tight and press your ejection button," said Prince Wayne. "Ok why didn't I think of that? One for the money, two for the show, three to get ready and four to go! Geronimoooo!" Into the water Prince Jerl landed safely, and Prince Mick waited on the beach. " Man do I owe Prince Wayne, I panicked and forgot all about my plan of escape," said Prince Jerl. That's what friends are for. We'll see him at the game.

After they both were dry and safe, they immediately rushed to the palace to check for results. La La Land had never been prettier and certainly never cleaner. Everything seemed to look sparkling brand new. "Princess Fee just has to feel better now," they thought. By the time they reached the castle, Princess Fee met them at the door. "My heroes", she shouted as she hugged them and kissed them.

"Ewwww," they exclaimed as they stood trapped in her embrace. "Just tell us you feel better," said Prince Mick. " I do, and I owe it all to you. Thank you for fighting those nasty bugs. You are very smart and very brave," said Princess Fee. "Ahhh, it was nothing. Right, Prince Mick?" "Roger," said Prince Mick. "Who's Roger?" asked Lady Erica. "Never mind," the boys sighed together. Let's play ball!!

"THE ROYAL KICKBALL GAME"

Objective:

This story is simply to enjoy. Team sports have been proven to teach a lot of leadership skills as well as post game etiquette. The main difference that should be noted is that while the home team will always win in La La Land, children should be prepared to cope with losses and disappointment in reality.

Suggestion:

This story could precede a little league event, a field day, or to cheer a child up after experiencing a first loss. Many great athletes imagined winning and pretended to break records before ever realizing their dreams.

Once upon a time in "La La Land," the hour had finally arrived! It was time for the Royal Kickball Game. Sit back and let your imagination guide you through every exciting game time sensation.

What a wonderful warm day it is as the smell of popcorn, hotdogs, and pizza fills the air. Then just as the hot, hot, hot sun has almost dried you out, the zesty zing of some crunchy, but sweet lemon ice will bring miracle relief without a doubt.

Suddenly the music starts…. Dun dun dun dun…yeah! The crowd begins to cheer. R-O-Y-A-L, our team is tough as a nail! Go team go! Go team go! It is always so awesome. First the visiting team comes out, representing "The Other Side" and boo's filled the air. The Other Side has some very good players, but they know who has home field advantage. This game is on the "Big V." "The Big V," named because of its shape, is in the middle of "La La Land" and was donated by the Royal Hough (Huff) Family. All challengers dreaded playing at such a high-tech facility, and if that wasn't enough, this was the biggest rivalry of the century. All of a sudden out of the distal end of the Big V, are loud fireworks and fog. Then out of the fog appears a long white stretched 4-runner with flashing lights. Sounding like a gigantic robot, he says: "My name is TRE' and I have the starting line up for the Royal Wild Wolfpack! Repeat, I have the starting line up for the Royal Wild Wolfpack."

From somewhere up 341 road #17, Prince Jerl! From the left point of the Big V, #14 Prince Wayne and #12 Prince Chris! From the right point of the Big V,#10 Princess Tonya! From the right top of the Big V, #3 Princess Tonie, #6 Princess Pam, All Region #11 Prince Mick and Co-Captain All American #18 Prince Dell! From the left top of the Big V, All Area, All Conference, Hustle Award Winning #13 Princess Fee! Last but not least, also from the top left of the V, the one, the only, All Conference, All Area, All Region, All State, All American, All Universe, Olympic Gold Medalist and team captain #21 Prince Celle!!! And the crowd goes wild. (cheering noises)

The National Anthem is rendered by the world famous La La Land Doll Baby Choir. Then the announcer yells let's play ball!

The Royal Wild Wolfpack wins the coin toss. They will be kicking first. The Other Side uses their toughest roller first, but Prince Mick will kick first for the Royal Wild Wolfpack. (kicking sound) And he's off! What a kick! This could be a home run (cheers). It is! It is! It is a home run.

The Royal Wild WolfPack takes an early lead on The Other Side. Next Princess Pam has a good kick and makes it to second base. Princess Tonya kicks and gets to first. Princess Tonie kicks and gets one base moving the others making the bases loaded. Now comes Princess Fee. She's still a little weak. **(Can you tighten your toes and concentrate really hard to help her get a good kick?)** Here Goes! Oh No! First roll is no good. Uh Oh! The second roll is a foul! (ahhhh**)(Ok everyone, clinch your fist and squeeze your toes really tight to help Princess Fee.)** Here Goes! Boom! She did it. We did it! It's way out there. The girls are running! Princess Pam comes in first! (Yeah) Princess Tonya scores behind her, and Princess Tonie rushes to home plate. (Yeah, Cheers). And… Hurry, Hurry… Looks like a grand slam. Princess Fee makes it in taking the score to 5-0! Yeah! (cheers) Prince Jerl kicked next and made it to third base. Prince Wayne kicks a pop up which is caught giving The Other Side their first out. Prince Chris makes it to first, but gets out on his attempt to steal to second base (ahhhh). Prince Dell has a big kick and gets to second base! Yeah! Now here comes Prince Celle. He is quite the playmaker. He modestly approaches the front waiting for a trick roll. Just as he suspected the roller puts a spin on the ball, but Prince Celle had mastered that type roll. He kicks the ball so far over the heads of The Other Side that Prince Jerl got home, Prince Dell got in and Prince Celle got in with scores with enough time to do his Royal Rough Tough Hough Homerun Dance! 8-0! Yeah! It's another blow out. The fans are having a blast.

The Royal Wild Wolfpack calls in their reserve kicker, the baby Prince Vic, just to give The Other Side their third out and a chance to score, but it's hopeless. No one has ever beaten The Royal Wild Wolfpack on the Big V in La La Land. They are the fastest, the strongest, and simply the best. After two rounds of three straight outs for both teams and four more runs for the Wild Wolfpack, The Other Side would have had enough. It's over! A 12-0 shut out!

What an awesome game! Everyone shakes hands, exchanges compliments and runs to the back yard for cookies and kool-aid (yey). While lingering back and savoring the moment Prince Celle shares, "you know what Princess Fee?" "What, Prince Celle?" "Winning really isn't everything . . . but it sure is fun!" Yes, It is Bro Bro, Yes It is.

"THE ROYAL WATER RIDE"

Objective:

To direct children's imagination to experience a wonderful, fantasy theme park ride featuring water, water and more WATER!

Suggestion:

This story could precede a first time visit to an amusement park, maybe a school field trip, or even a family vacation. Also it can be helpful before a lesson on water safety, the necessity of water to survival, marine biology and aquatic life.

Once upon a time in La La Land, the Royal Family was next in line for the super sensational spectacular soaking rooty tooty casplashooty Royal Water Ride. Princess Fee is about to explode with excitement. Lady Erica is not too thrilled but faithful enough to Princess Fee to fearfully tag along. Prince Vic and Prince Celle are excellent swimmers and are almost as excited as Princess Fee. " Yey! Here it comes! Here it comes!" she cheered.

The Big Bubble Banana Boat pulls in full of happy screaming children yelling "one more time," but only just for fun because they understood that they must take turns after two rounds. "Ok, all aboard! All aboard," said the driver as his assistants fastened everyone's seat belts and life jackets. Suddenly there's what sounds like air leaking from a gigantic balloon. It is the mist machine. Shhh! Shhh! All the children scream with excitement from the chill of the cold mist and the thrill of knowing this always happens just before the ride starts (screams). **(Do you know what cool mist is? It's like standing with the freezer door open. Have you ever done that?)** Well fasten your pretend seatbelt and grab your imagination. We are about to depart from the Royal Water Ride station.

First everyone's anticipating the deep drop… and it happens! (screams) We're off! A fifteen foot drop into a current pool shaped like a humongous zig zag lazy river.

This water rushes the big boat under five waterfalls and as if everyone's not soaked enough, it then slides quickly around a curve to break seven whopping waves from the simulated ocean shore. The whopping waves wash the boat over five huge hills and at the bottom of the last hill is a large blue underwater tunnel. The Big Bubble Banana Boat slows down to give riders an under water view of an aquarium filled with the world's most beautiful and colorful fish. What colors do you see? Describe the different fish and the shapes of the fish you see. Look quickly... the boat will begin to speed up soon. Ok, here goes! (zoom!, screams!)

The Big Bubble Banana Boat takes off and speeds down an eight-story drop before taking two loops, three twists, one more loop and six splash circles. After the last splash circle, the big boat drives into another wave pool to take on nine waves and heads for the final fantastic waterfall finish.

There it is! The grand finale. The boat speeds up as it hurries up hill preparing to splash the very tall, but mini Niagara Falls. Blast Off! (screams, Whoa) Another nine story drop leading into a loop to loop-to-loop drop right through the huge waterfall. Wow! Yey! One more time!

"Awesome ride", thought Princess Fee as the boat approached the station. "It is so nice they have to let you ride it twice. This Royal Water Ride has to be the greatest water ride on earth," she said. "Yeah", sighed Prince Celle and Prince Vic together. "That was cool," they continued and with a gigantic group grin they yelled in unison, "Again! Again!"

"THE ROYAL TASTE TEST"

Objective:

This story is to stimulate the senses and to motivate the minds of youngsters to be more inquisitive about the many types of foods.

Suggestions:

An actual taste test would be awesome following this poem. This poem can be used before, or after a lesson on the digestive track, including specifically the function of the tongue, taste buds and saliva. This can also be used to introduce different food groups and possibly the food pyramid found in most food and nutrition textbooks.

Once upon a time in "La La Land", it was time for the Royal Taste Test. Everyone was in their place and ready to do their very best. With all their tongues and tummies ready to grub, it didn't matter if they started with a delicious dessert or a super sub. Have you ever been to a taste test? It's so much fun for everyone, especially if your challenge is a cinnamon bun. The rules are simple, and there are only three. You must know them to follow them. Now what could they be?

Rules: 1. Close your eyes.

2. Taste and guess times three, then

3. Open your eyes so you can see.

If you like what you taste, be sure to share, but not to shout. If you don't like it, use your good manners to cover your mouth and in a napkin spit it out! No harm is done, and no one's offended, and all of the fun continues as intended. Are you ready? Are you set? Let's go! Grab your imagination and let the foods flow.

Big Boy and Beauty are first in line. Any time is a good time for them to dine. "Umm umm good," they grunt as they started licking. Puppy and Downy think they should have the next picking. Pretty Bear is always hoping for cookies, while MJ and Starks sniff for a doughnut ring. It really doesn't matter for the cute little Sweetie since she and Bing will eat anything. Pickles, peaches, plums, and pumpkin pie, hamburger, hot dogs, ham or spam; slurpies, soda pop, soup, sausages and strawberry pancakes stacked high. Sweet and sour, bitter, spicy and hot, hot, was your challenge something you could describe or not?

It is always fun to return and try again after you've taken a rest. It's always a surprise, kind of like show and tell, but instead it's "taste and smell," at the Royal Taste Test.

"THE ROYAL TALENT SHOW"

Objective:

This poem is to inspire children to look within themselves for their own special talent. They are all gifted and they must be encouraged to find that one thing that they feel makes them feel proud to be special and unique from all others. It is also important that they learn to appreciate the talents and differences of others.

Suggestion:

This short story poem can help prevent, or ward off butterflies before a special performance at church, school, or in the community. It may also help children realize that anything they are good at can be considered a talent, so there is never a need to feel belittled, or inferior to anyone else for any reason. It also plants a seed of need to give thanks to God for all the gifts that they have been blessed with.

Once upon a time in "La La Land".... it was time for the Royal Talent Show. People would come from all around to experience the joy, laughter, and the sounds. The ones you least expect were often the acts that shined. Yet, really how great or how small it really didn't matter as long as for fun it was defined. You really have to be there to fully appreciate the celebration. Lady Erica is always the hostess and she can lead anyone there that has a great imagination.

The first act includes Charlie Owl singing "Human Nature" by Michael Jackson and then Master Brain break dances to " Beat It," which is also a popular Jackson tune. Lady Ronica and Lady Natalie sing a duet about the moon shinning over a sand dune. Prince Celle does a drum solo and Prince Vic sings a romantic ballad. Prince Dell plays an original keyboard arrangement, while Lady Monique tries to eat the world's largest salad! Princess Pam, Princess Londi and Princess Tonya do an African dance, so Prince Mick decides that he wants a chance. He declares he can hit twenty-five free throws straight

after spinning on his head and even though he just ate. Oh boy, He does it! He does it! Hoo ray! Hoo ray! Then Lady Nicky and Lady Natalie and Lady Monique do a very short play. Next Prince Wayne does a very cool rap. Princess Tonie demonstrates how she makes her beautiful grass dolls as Princess Fee demonstrates how to take the perfect nap.

So much, so much, so much fun; if you could have been there what would you have done? **(Pause to get response)** Well before everyone goes home, it never mattered how long. No one ever wants to leave before hearing the final song. A winner is never declared, just lots of fun for free, but if there had to be a winner it would be the grand finale. The world famous "Doll Baby Choir" led by Princess Fee always sings a powerful praise song and shouts the victory.

Soon all the participants and audience joins in and they have a time you know, and that's the way it always ends at the "Royal Talent Show".

THE END

CONCLUSION

It is my prayer that this book will help parents and teachers inspire children to use their imagination. This skill contributes not only to a child's neurological and intellectual development, but it gives a more "old fashion" form of escape from the high tech, but too often corrupt society that we live in. Of course we must keep them in touch with reality, but unfortunately many children do not deserve the horrible realities they must prematurely face. If this book, along with prayer can be a tool to offer temporary escape versus temporary insanity then its purpose would have been fulfilled. May God grant each reader, teacher, parent, and child the reality of his or her sweetest dreams.

Felecia Reneé Hough, RN-BSN

SPECIAL THANKS

To God for saving me at an early age.

To all of my cousins, but especially my dearest playmates Jerl, Mickey, and Cordell, I will forever treasure your friendship and memories.

To Najah Clemmons, Brandon Clark, and Kelly Hough for your labored time and efforts to illustrate my childhood dreams.

To Mrs. Gail Hall for putting the music in my head on paper.

And all of the following people who in some way inspired, encouraged, or assisted me to begin and complete this project.

Cynthia Mungo	Pamela R. Hough
Margret Lawhorn	Miles Gardner
Claude Ellis	Donna Brand
Angela G. McIver	Shirley Halley
Supt. William A. Prioleau	Dr. Wayne P. Smith
Margaree Rich	Pat Shultz
Tracey Ratchford	Rufus Hough
Bishop Patrick Wooden	Nancy Ward
Supt. James L. Lee	Bishop Johnny James Johnson
Tonie Baldwin	Emma Scott